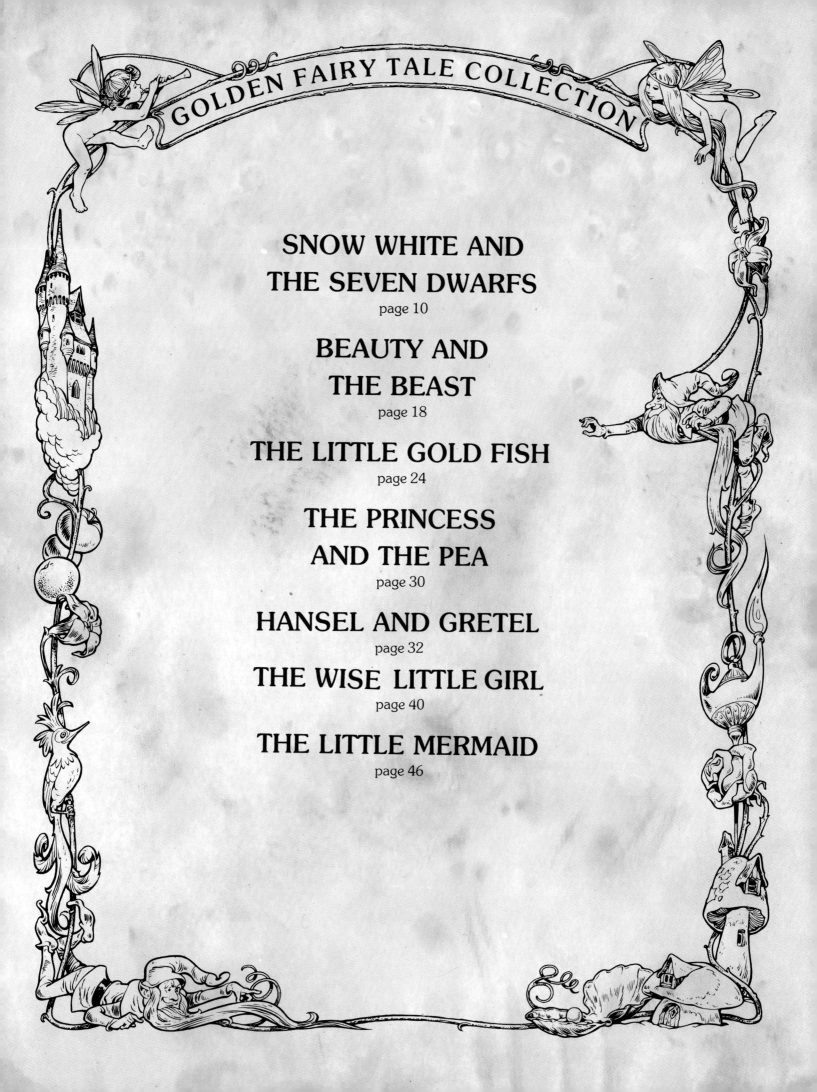

GOLDEN FAIRY TALE COLLECTION

ILLUSTRATED BY TONY WOLF
TEXT BY PETER HOLEINONE

© DAMI EDITORE , ITALY

First published in the United States 1990
by Gallery Books, an imprint of W. H. Smith Publishers, Inc.,
112 Madison Avenue, New York, New York 10016.

Gallery Books are available for bulk purchase for sales
promotions and premium use. For details write or telephone
the Manager of Special Sales, W. H. Smith Publishers, Inc.,
112 Madison Avenue, New York, New York 10016. (212) 532-6600

PRINTED BY
ARTI GRAFICHE MOTTA
MILANO - ITALY

The story of
SNOW WHITE
and other tales

GALLERY BOOKS
An Imprint of W. H. Smith Publishers Inc.
112 Madison Avenue
New York, New York 10016

Once upon a time . . .

. . . a little girl called Snow White was abandoned in the forest by her wicked stepmother. By chance, she met seven dwarfs, and this story is all about them . . .

SNOW WHITE AND THE SEVEN DWARFS

Once upon a time . . . in a great castle, a Prince's daughter grew up happy and contented, in spite of a jealous stepmother. She was very pretty, with blue eyes and long black hair. Her skin was delicate and fair, and so she was called Snow White. Everyone was quite sure she would become very beautiful. Though her stepmother was a wicked woman, she too was very beautiful, and the magic mirror told her this every day, whenever she asked it.

"Mirror, mirror on the wall, who is the loveliest lady in the land?" The reply was always; "You are, your Majesty," until the dreadful day when she heard it say, "Snow White is the loveliest in the land." The stepmother was furious and, wild with jealousy, began plotting to get rid of her rival. Calling one of her trusty servants, she bribed him with a rich reward to take Snow White into the forest, far away from the Castle. Then, unseen, he was to put her to death. The greedy servant, attracted to the reward, agreed to do this deed, and he led the innocent little girl away. However, when they came to the fatal spot, the man's courage failed him and, leaving Snow White sitting beside a tree, he mumbled an excuse and ran off. Snow White was all alone in the forest.

Night came, but the servant did not return. Snow White, alone in the dark forest, began to cry bitterly. She thought she could feel terrible eyes spying on her, and she heard strange sounds and rustlings that made her heart thump. At last, overcome by tiredness, she fell asleep curled under a tree.

Snow White slept fitfully, wakening from time to time with a start and staring into the darkness round her. Several times, she thought she felt something, or somebody touch her as she slept.

At last, dawn woke the forest to the song of the birds, and Snow White too, awoke. A whole world was stirring to life and the little girl was glad to see how silly her fears had been. However, the thick trees were like a wall round her, and as she tried to find out where she was, she came upon a path. She walked along it, hopefully. On she walked till she came to a clearing. There stood a strange cottage, with a tiny door, tiny windows and a tiny chimney pot. Everything about the cottage was much tinier than it ought to be. Snow White pushed the door open.

"I wonder who lives here?" she said to herself, peeping round the kitchen. "What tiny plates! And spoons! There must be seven of them, the table's laid for seven people." Upstairs was a bedroom with seven neat little beds. Going back to the kitchen, Snow White had an idea.

"I'll make them something to eat. When they come home, they'll be glad to find a meal ready." Towards dusk, seven tiny men marched homewards singing. But when they opened the door to their surprise, they found a bowl of hot steaming soup on the table, and the whole house spick and span. Upstairs was Snow White, fast asleep on one of the beds. The chief dwarf prodded her gently.

"Who are you?" he asked. Snow White told them her sad story, and tears sprang to the dwarfs' eyes. Then one of them said, as he noisily blew his nose:

"Stay here with us!"

"Hooray! Hooray!" they cheered, dancing joyfully round the little girl. The dwarfs said to Snow White:

"You can live here and tend to the house while we're down the mine. Don't worry about your stepmother leaving you in the forest. We love you and *we'll* take care of you!" Snow White gratefully accepted their hospitality, and next morning the dwarfs set off for work. But they warned Snow White not to open the door to strangers.

Meanwhile, the servant had returned to the castle, with the heart of a roe deer. He gave it to the cruel stepmother, telling her it belonged to Snow White, so that he could claim the reward. Highly pleased, the stepmother turned again to the magic mirror. But her hopes were dashed, for the mirror replied: "The loveliest in the land is still Snow White, who lives in the seven dwarfs' cottage, down in the forest." The stepmother was beside herself with rage.

"She must die! She must die!" she screamed. Disguising herself as an old peasant woman, she put a poisoned apple with the others in her basket. Then, taking the quickest way into the forest, she rowed across the marsh at the edge of the trees. She reached the bank unseen, just as Snow White stood waving goodbye to the seven dwarfs on their way to the mine.

Snow White was in the kitchen when she heard the sound at the door: KNOCK! KNOCK!

"Who's there?" she called suspiciously, remembering the dwarfs' advice.

"I'm an old peasant woman selling apples," came the reply.

"I don't need any apples, thank you," she replied.

"But they are beautiful apples and ever so juicy!" said the velvety voice from outside the door.

"I'm not supposed to open the door to anyone," said the little girl, who was reluctant to disobey her friends.

"And quite right too! Good girl! If you promised not to open up to strangers, then of course you can't buy. You *are* a good girl indeed!" Then the old woman went on.

"And as a reward for being good, I'm going to make you a gift of one of my apples!" Without a further thought, Snow White opened the door just a tiny crack, to take the apple.

"There! Now isn't that a nice apple?" Snow White bit into the fruit, and as she did, fell to the ground in a faint: the effect of the terrible poison left her lifeless instantaneously. Now chuckling evilly, the wicked stepmother hurried off, while Snow White turned white as a sheet with the paleness of death. One of the rabbits who had witnessed the scene ran with the other animals to tell the dwarfs.

"Come quickly! Snow White is dead!" The dwarfs rushed breathlessly to the cottage.

"What happened?" they gasped in despair.

"An old woman knocked at the door and . . ." The seven dwarfs did their best to bring Snow White round, but still she lay, white and lifeless. The angry dwarfs asked the animals which way the witch had gone. They had almost caught up with her when a sudden flash of lightning ripped the sky. It struck the crag where the witch was standing, and she toppled over the precipice.

Now that the witch was dead, the dwarfs went back to the cottage. They wept for a long time over Snow White, and laid her on a bed of rose petals. Then they carried her into the forest and put her into a crystal coffin.

Each day they laid a flower there.

Then one evening, they discovered a strange young man admiring Snow White's lovely face through the glass. After listening to the story, the Prince (for he was a prince!) made a suggestion.

"If you allow me to take her to the Castle, I'll call in famous doctors to waken her from this peculiar sleep. She's so lovely . . . I'd love to kiss her. . . !" He did, and as though by magic, the Prince's kiss broke the spell. To everyone's astonishment, Snow White opened her eyes. She had amazingly come back to life! Now in love, the Prince asked Snow White to marry him, and the dwarfs had reluctantly to say goodbye to Snow White.

From that day on, Snow White lived happily in a great castle. But from time to time, she was drawn back to visit the little cottage down in the forest.

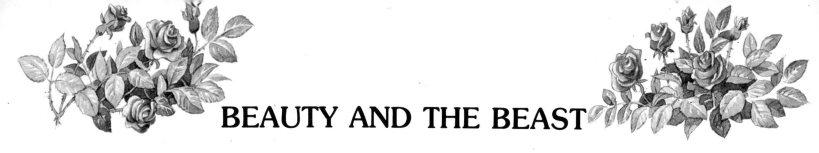

BEAUTY AND THE BEAST

Once upon a time . . . as a merchant set off for market, he asked each of his three daughters what she would like as a present on his return. The first daughter wanted a brocade dress, the second a pearl necklace, but the third, whose name was Beauty, the youngest, prettiest and sweetest of them all, said to her father:

"All I'd like is a rose you've picked specially for me!"

When the merchant had finished his business, he set off for home. However, a sudden storm blew up, and his horse could hardly make headway in the howling gale. Cold and weary, the merchant had lost all hope of reaching an inn when he suddenly noticed a bright light shining in the middle of a wood. As he drew near, he saw that it was a castle, bathed in light.

"I hope I'll find shelter there for the night," he said to himself. When he reached the door, he saw it was open, but though he shouted, nobody came to greet him. Plucking up courage, he went inside, still calling out to attract attention. On a table in the main hall, a splendid dinner lay already served. The merchant lingered, still shouting for the owner of the castle. But no-one came, and so the starving merchant sat down to a hearty meal.

Overcome by curiosity, he ventured upstairs, where the corridor led into magnificent rooms and halls. A fire crackled in the first room and a soft bed looked very inviting. It was now late, and the merchant could not resist. He lay down on the bed and fell fast asleep. When he woke next morning, an unknown hand had placed a mug of steaming coffee and some fruit by his bedside.

The merchant had breakfast and after tidying himself up, went downstairs to thank his generous host. But, as on the evening before, there was nobody in sight. Shaking his head in wonder at the strangeness of it all, he went towards the garden where he had left his horse, tethered to a tree. Suddenly, a large rose bush caught his eye.

Remembering his promise to Beauty, he bent down to pick a rose. Instantly, out of the rose garden, sprang a horrible beast, wearing splendid clothes. Two bloodshot eyes, gleaming angrily, glared at him and a deep, terrifying voice growled: "Ungrateful man! I gave you shelter, you ate at my table and slept in my own bed, but now all the thanks I get is the theft of my favourite flowers! I shall put you to death for this slight!" Trembling with fear, the merchant fell on his knees before the Beast.

"Forgive me! Forgive me! Don't kill me! I'll do anything you say! The rose wasn't for me, it was for my daughter Beauty. I promised to bring her back a rose from my journey!" The Beast dropped the paw it had clamped on the unhappy merchant.

"I shall spare your life, but on one condition, that you bring me your daughter!" The terror-stricken merchant, faced with certain death if he did not obey, promised that he would do so. When he reached home in tears, his three daughters ran to greet him. After he had told them of his dreadful adventure, Beauty put his mind at rest immediately.

"Dear father, I'd do anything for you! Don't worry, you'll be able to keep your promise and save your life! Take me to the castle. I'll stay there in your place!" The merchant hugged his daughter.

"I never did doubt your love for me. For the moment I can only thank you for saving my life." So Beauty was led to the castle. The Beast, however, had quite an unexpected greeting for the girl. Instead of menacing doom as it had done with her father, it was surprisingly pleasant.

In the beginning, Beauty was frightened of the Beast, and shuddered at the sight of it. Then she found that, in spite of the monster's awful head, her horror of it was gradually fading as time went by. She had one of the finest rooms in the Castle, and sat for hours, embroidering in front of the fire. And the Beast would sit, for hours on end, only a short distance away, silently gazing at her.

Then it started to say a few kind words, till in the end, Beauty was amazed to discover that she was actually enjoying its conversation. The days passed, and Beauty and the Beast became good friends. Then one day, the Beast asked the girl to be his wife.

Taken by surprise, Beauty did not know what to say. Marry such an ugly monster? She would rather die! But she did not want to hurt the feelings of one who, after all, had been kind to her. And she remembered too that she owed it her own life as well as her father's.

"I really can't say yes," she began shakily. "I'd so much like to . . ." The Beast interrupted her with an abrupt gesture.

"I quite understand! And I'm not offended by your refusal!" Life went on as usual, and nothing further was said. One day, the Beast presented Beauty with a magnificent magic mirror. When Beauty peeped into it, she could see her family, far away.

"You won't feel so lonely now," were the words that accompanied the gift. Beauty stared for hours at her distant family. Then she began to feel worried. One day, the Beast found her weeping beside the magic mirror.

"What's wrong?" he asked, kindly as always.

"My father is gravely ill and close to dying! Oh, how I wish I could see him again, before it's too late!" But the Beast only shook its head.

"No! You will never leave this castle!" And off it stalked in a rage. However, a little later, it returned and spoke solemnly to the girl.

"If you swear that you will return here in seven days time, I'll let you go and visit your father!" Beauty threw herself at the Beast's feet in delight.

"I swear! I swear I will! How kind you are! You've made a loving daughter so happy!" In reality, the merchant had fallen ill from a broken heart at knowing his daughter was being kept prisoner. When he embraced her again, he was soon on the road to recovery. Beauty stayed beside him for hours on end, describing her life at the Castle, and explaining that the Beast was really good and kind. The days flashed past, and at last the merchant was able to leave his bed. He was completely well again. Beauty was happy at last. However, she had failed to notice that seven days had gone by.

Then one night she woke from a terrible nightmare. She had dreamt that the Beast was dying and calling for her, twisting in agony.

"Come back! Come back to me!" it was pleading. The solemn promise she had made drove her to leave home immediately.

"Hurry! Hurry, good horse!" she said, whipping her steed onwards towards the castle, afraid that she might arrive too late. She rushed up the stairs, calling, but there was no reply. Her heart in her mouth, Beauty ran into the garden and there crouched the Beast, its eyes shut, as though dead. Beauty threw herself at it and hugged it tightly.

"Don't die! Don't die! I'll marry you . . ." At these words, a miracle took place. The Beast's ugly snout turned magically into the face of a handsome young man.

"How I've been longing for this moment!" he said. "I was suffering in silence, and couldn't tell my frightful secret. An evil witch turned me into a monster and only the love of a maiden willing to accept me as I was, could transform me back into my real self. My dearest! I'll be so happy if you'll marry me . . ."

The wedding took place shortly after and, from that day on, the young Prince would have nothing but roses in his gardens. And that's why, to this day, the castle is known as the Castle of the Rose.

THE LITTLE GOLD FISH

Once upon a time . . . a poor fisherman lived in a humble cottage near the sea. One day, he set off as usual with his load of nets to go fishing.

"Don't you dare come home empty-handed!" shouted his nagging wife from the door. Down on the shore, he had just thrown the nets into the sea, when something glittering in the meshes caught his eye.

"What a strange fish!" he said to himself, picking up a golden-yellow fish. And his amazement grew when he heard the fish say these words:

"Kind fisherman, let me go free! I'm the son of the Sea King, and if you let me go, I'll grant any wish you care to make!" Alarmed at this miracle, without a second thought, the fisherman tossed the fish back into the water. But when he went home and told his wife what had happened she scolded him soundly:

"What! When the fish said your wishes could come true, you should have asked it for something! Go back to the beach and if you see it, ask for a new washtub! Just look at the state of ours!"

The poor man went back to the shore. As soon as he called the fish, it popped up from the water.

"Were you calling me? Here I am!" it said. The fisherman explained what his wife wanted, and the fish quickly replied:

"You were very good to me! Go home, and you'll see that your wish has come true!" Certain that his wife would be pleased, the fisherman hurried home. But the minute he opened the door, his wife screeched:

"So it really is a magic fish that you allowed to go free! Just look at that old washtub! It's brand new! But if that little fish has such powers, you can't possibly be content with such a miserable little wish! Go straight back and get it to give you a new house!"

The fisherman hurried back to the shore.

"I wonder if I'll see it again! I hope it hasn't gone away! Little fish! Little fish!" he began to call from the water's edge.

"Here I am! What do you want this time?" he heard it ask.

"Well, my wife would like . . ."

"I can imagine!" remarked the fish. "And what does she want now?"

"A big house!" murmured the fisherman, hesitantly.

"All right! You were kind to me and you shall have your wish!" The fisherman lingered on the way home, enjoying the feeling of making his wife happy with a new house. The roof of the splendid new house was already in sight, when his wife rushed

up to him in a fury.

"Look here! Now that we know how really powerful this fish is, we can't be content with only a house! We must ask for more! Run back and ask for a real palace, not an ordinary house like this one! And fine clothes! And jewels too!" The fisherman was quite upset. However, he had been henpecked for so many years that he was unable to say "no",

so he trudged back to the water's edge. Full of doubts, he called the little fish, but it was some time before it leapt from the waves. In the meantime, the sea had begun to foam . . .

"I'm sorry to trouble you again, but my wife has had second thoughts, and she'd like a fine palace, and . . . and also . . ." Again the little fish granted the fisherman his wishes, but he

seemed less friendly than before. At last, relieved at having been able to see his wife's desires fulfilled, the good fisherman turned homewards. Home was now a magnificent palace. How wonderful it was! At the top of a flight of steps leading to the palace, stood his wife, dressed like a great lady and dripping with jewels, impatiently waiting for him.

"Go back and ask for . . ." But the fisherman broke in:

"What? Such a fine palace! We must be content with what we have! Don't you think that's asking too much? . . ."

"Go back, I said! Do as you're told! And ask the fish to make me an Empress!" The poor fisherman set off unhappily for the seashore. In the meantime, a storm had blown up. The sky was black and terrible flashes of lightning lit the darkness, while the waves crashed angrily on the beach. Kneeling on the rock amidst the spray, in a low voice the fisherman began to call the little fish. And when it came, he told it his wife's latest request. But this time, after listening in silence, the little gold fish disappeared beneath the waves without saying a word. And though the fisherman waited, the little fish never came back. A great flash of lightning, much brighter than all the others lit up the sky, and the fisherman saw that both the new house and the palace had vanished without trace. The humble old cottage stood where it had always been. But this time, his wife was waiting for him in tears.

"It serves you right! We should have been pleased with what we had, instead of always asking for more!" grumbled the fisherman angrily.But in the depths of his heart, he was glad that everything had gone back to normal.

Next day and every day, he went back to his fishing, but he never saw the little goldfish again.

THE PRINCESS AND THE PEA

Once upon a time . . . there was a prince who, after wandering the land searching for a wife, returned to his castle and told his unhappy parents that he had been unable to find a bride.

Now, this young man was difficult to please, and he had not been greatly taken with any of the noble young ladies he had met on his travels. He was looking for a bride who was not only beautiful, but also well-born, with the elegance and manners found only in those of noble birth and background.

One evening, during a fierce hurricane that had suddenly blown up, a persistent knocking was heard at the castle door. The prince's father sent a servant to find out who was there. Standing on the steps, lit by flashes of lightning, in the driving rain, was a young lady. "I'm a princess," she said, "seeking shelter for myself and my page. My carriage has broken down and the coachman can't repair it till tomorrow."

In the meantime, the prince's mother had appeared to welcome the guest. She stared disapprovingly at the girl's muddy wet garments, and decided to find out if she really was of gentle birth.

"Prepare a soft soft bed in the Blue Room," she said, "I'll come myself and make sure everything is in order." She told the servants to lay a pile of soft quilts on top of the mattress, and under the mattress she hid a pea. Then she showed the girl to her room. The rain beat down all night and lightning streaked the sky. In the morning, the prince's mother asked her guest: "Did you sleep well? Was the bed comfortable?" The girl politely replied:

"It was a lovely soft bed, so soft that I could feel something hard under the mattress. This morning, I discovered it was a pea. It kept me awake all night!" The prince's mother offered her apologies, before rushing off to her son.

"A real princess at last! Just think! She could feel the pea I hid under the mattress! Now, only a well-born lady could do that!"

The prince had finally found the bride of his dreams. After the wedding, the pea was placed inside a gold and crystal box and exhibited in the castle museum.

HANSEL AND GRETEL

Once upon a time . . . a very poor woodcutter lived in a tiny cottage in the forest with his two children, Hansel and Gretel. His second wife often ill-treated the children and was forever nagging the woodcutter.

"There is not enough food in the house for us all. There are too many mouths to feed! We must get rid of the two brats," she declared. And she kept on trying to persuade her husband to abandon his children in the forest.

"Take them miles from home, so far that they can never find their way back! Maybe someone will find them and give them a home." The downcast woodcutter didn't know what to do. Hansel who, one evening, had overheard his parents' conversation, comforted Gretel.

"Don't worry! If they do leave us in the forest, we'll find the way home," he said. And slipping out of the house he filled his pockets with little white pebbles, then went back to bed.

All night long, the woodcutter's wife harped on and on at her husband till, at dawn, he led Hansel and Gretel away into the forest. But as they went into the depths of the trees, Hansel dropped a little white pebble here and there on the mossy green ground. At a certain point, the two children found they really were alone: the woodcutter had plucked up enough courage to desert them, had mumbled an excuse and was gone.

Night fell but the woodcutter did not return. Gretel began to sob bitterly. Hansel too felt scared but he tried to hide his feelings and comfort his sister.

"Don't cry, trust me! I swear I'll take you home, even if Father doesn't come back for us!" Luckily the moon was full that night and Hansel waited till its cold light filtered through the trees.

"Now give me your hand!" he said. "We'll get home safely, you'll see!" The tiny white pebbles gleamed in the moonlight, and the children found their way home. They crept through a half-open window, without wakening their parents. Cold, tired but thankful to be home again, they slipped into bed.

Next day, when their stepmother discovered that Hansel and Gretel had returned, she went into a rage. Stifling her anger in front of the children, she locked her bedroom door, reproaching her husband for failing to carry out her orders. The weak woodcutter protested, torn as he was between shame and fear of disobeying his cruel wife. The wicked stepmother kept Hansel and Gretel under lock and key all day with nothing for supper but a sip of water and some hard bread. All night, husband and wife quarrelled, and when dawn came, the woodcutter led the children out into the forest.

Hansel, however, had not eaten his bread, and as he walked through the trees, he left a trail of crumbs behind him to mark the way. But the little boy had forgotten about the hungry birds that lived in the forest. When they saw him, they flew along behind and in no time at all, had eaten all the crumbs. Again, with a lame excuse, the woodcutter left his two children by themselves.

"I've left a trail, like last time!" Hansel whispered to Gretel, consolingly. But when night fell, they saw to their horror, that all the crumbs had gone.

"I'm frightened!" wept Gretel bitterly. "I'm cold and hungry and I want to go home!"

"Don't be afraid. I'm here to look after you!" Hansel tried to encourage his sister, but he too shivered when he glimpsed frightening shadows and evil eyes around them in the darkness. All night the two children huddled together for warmth at the foot of a large tree.

When dawn broke, they started to wander about the forest, seeking a path, but all hope soon faded. They were well and truly lost. On they walked and walked, till suddenly they came upon a strange cottage in the middle of a glade.

"This is chocolate!" gasped Hansel as he broke a lump of plaster from the wall.

"And this is icing!" exclaimed Gretel, putting another piece of wall in her mouth. Starving but delighted, the children began to eat pieces of candy broken off the cottage.

"Isn't this delicious?" said Gretel, with her mouth full. She had never tasted anything so nice.

"We'll stay here," Hansel declared, munching a bit of nougat. They were just about to try a piece of the biscuit door when it quietly swung open.

"Well, well!" said an old woman, peering out with a crafty look. "And haven't you children a sweet tooth?"

"Come in! Come in, you've nothing to fear!" went on the old woman. Unluckily for Hansel and Gretel, however, the sugar candy cottage belonged to an old witch, her trap for catching unwary victims. The two children had come to a really nasty place . . .

"You're nothing but skin and bone!" said the witch, locking Hansel into a cage. "I shall fatten you up and eat you!"

"You can do the housework," she told Gretel grimly, "then I'll make a meal of you too!" As luck would have it, the witch had very bad eyesight, and when Gretel smeared butter on her glasses, she could see even less.

"Let me feel your finger!" said the witch to Hansel every day, to check if he was getting any fatter. Now, Gretel had brought her brother a chicken bone, and when the witch went to touch his finger, Hansel held out the bone.

"You're still much too thin!" she complained. "When will you become plump?" One day the witch grew tired of waiting.

"Light the oven," she told Gretel. "We're going to have a tasty roasted boy today!" A little later, hungry and impatient, she went on: "Run and see if the oven is hot enough." Gretel returned, whimpering: "I can't tell if it is hot enough or not." Angrily, the witch screamed at the little girl: "Useless child! All right, I'll see for myself." But when the witch bent down to peer inside the oven and check the heat, Gretel gave her a tremendous push and slammed the oven door shut. The witch had come to a fit and proper end. Gretel ran to set her brother free and they made quite sure that the oven door was tightly shut behind the witch. Indeed, just to be on the safe side, they fastened it firmly with a large padlock. Then they stayed for several days to eat some more of the house, till they discovered amongst the witch's belongings, a huge chocolate egg. Inside lay a casket of gold coins.

"The witch is now burnt to a cinder," said Hansel, "so we'll take this treasure with us." They filled a large basket with food and set off into the forest to search for the way home. This time, luck was with them, and on the second day, they saw their father come out of the house towards them, weeping.

"Your stepmother is dead. Come home with me now, my dear children!" The two children hugged the woodcutter.

"Promise you'll never ever desert us again," said Gretel, throwing her arms round her father's neck. Hansel opened the casket.

"Look, Father! We're rich now . . . You'll never have to chop wood again . . ."

And they all lived happily together ever after.

THE WISE LITTLE GIRL

Once upon a time . . . in the immense Russian steppe, lay a little village where nearly all the inhabitants bred horses. It was the month of October, when a big livestock market was held yearly in the main town. Two brothers, one rich and the other one poor, set off for market. The rich man rode a stallion, and the poor brother a young mare.

At dusk, they stopped beside an empty hut and tethered their horses outside, before going to sleep themselves on two heaps of straw. Great was their surprise, when, next morning they saw *three* horses outside, instead of two. Well, to be exact the newcomer was not really a *horse*. It was a foal, to which the mare had given birth during the night. Soon it had the strength to struggle to its feet, and after a drink of its mother's milk, the foal staggered its first few steps. The stallion greeted it with a cheerful whinny, and when the two brothers set eyes on it for the first time, the foal was standing beside the stallion.

"It belongs to me!" exclaimed Dimitri, the rich brother, the minute he saw it. "It's my stallion's foal." Ivan, the poor brother, began to laugh.

"Whoever heard of a stallion having a foal? It was born to my mare!"

"No, that's not true! It was standing close to the stallion, so it's the stallion's foal. And therefore it's mine!" The brothers started to quarrel,

then they decided to go to town and bring the matter before the judges. Still arguing, they headed for the big square where the courtroom stood. But what they didn't know was that it was a special day, the day when, once a year, the Emperor himself administered the law. He himself received all who came seeking justice. The brothers were ushered into his presence, and they told him all about the dispute.

Of course, the Emperor knew perfectly well who was the owner of the foal. He was on the point of proclaiming in favour of the poor brother, when suddenly Ivan developed an unfortunate twitch in his eye. The Emperor was greatly annoyed by this familiarity by a humble peasant, and decided to punish Ivan for his disrespect. After listening to both sides of the story, he declared it was difficult, indeed impossible, to say exactly who was the foal's rightful owner. And being in the mood for a spot of fun, and since he loved posing riddles and solving them as well, to the amusement of his counsellors, he exclaimed:

"I can't judge which of you should have the foal, so it will be awarded to whichever of you solves the following four riddles: what is the fastest thing in the world? What is the fattest? What's the softest and what is the most precious? I command you to return to the palace in a week's time with your answers!" Dimitri started to puzzle over the answers as soon as he left the courtroom. When he reached home, however, he realised he had nobody to help him.

"Well, I'll just have to seek help, for if I can't solve these riddles, I'll lose the foal!" Then he remembered a woman, one of his neighbours, to whom he had once lent a silver ducat. That had been some time ago, and with the interest, the neighbour now owed him *three* ducats. And since she had a reputation for being quick-witted, but also very astute, he decided to ask her advice, in exchange for cancelling part of her debt. But the woman was not slow to show how astute she really was, and promptly demanded that the whole debt be wiped out in exchange for the answers.

"The fastest thing in the world is my husband's bay horse," she said. "Nothing can beat it! The fattest is our pig! Such a huge beast has never been seen! The softest is the quilt I made for the bed, using my own goose's feathers. It's the envy of all my friends. The most precious thing in the world is my three-month old nephew. There isn't a more handsome child. I wouldn't exchange him for all the gold on earth, and that makes him the most precious thing on earth!"

Dimitri was rather doubtful about the woman's answers being correct. On the other hand, he had to take some kind of solution back to the Emperor. And he guessed, quite rightly, that if he didn't, he would be punished.

In the meantime, Ivan, who was a widower, had gone back to the humble cottage where he lived with his small daughter. Only seven years old, the little girl was often left alone, and as a result, was thoughtful and very clever for her age. The poor man took the little girl into his confidence, for like his brother, he knew he would never be able to find the answers by himself. The child sat in silence for a moment, then firmly said:

"Tell the Emperor that the fastest thing in the world is the cold north wind in winter. The fattest is the soil in our fields whose crops give life to men and animals alike, the softest thing is a child's caress and the most precious is honesty."

The day came when the two brothers were to return before the Emperor. They were led into his presence. The Emperor was curious to hear what they had to say, but he roared with laughter at Dimitri's foolish answers. However, when it was Ivan's turn to speak, a frown spread over the Emperor's face. The poor brother's wise replies made him squirm, especially the last one, about honesty, the most precious thing of all. The Emperor knew perfectly well that he had been dishonest in his dealings with the poor brother, for he had denied him justice. But he could not bear to admit it in front of his own counsellors, so he angrily demanded:

"Who gave you these answers?" Ivan told the Emperor that it was his small daughter. Still annoyed, the great man said:

43

"You shall be rewarded for having such a wise and clever daughter. You shall be awarded the foal that your brother claimed, together with a hundred silver ducats . . . But . . . but . . ." and the Emperor winked at his counsellors:

"You will come before me in seven days' time, bringing your daughter. And since she's so clever, she must appear before me neither naked nor dressed, neither on foot nor on horseback, neither bearing gifts nor empty-handed. And if she does this, you will have your reward. If not, you'll have your head chopped off for your impudence!"

The onlookers began to laugh, knowing that the poor man would never to able to fulfill the Emperor's conditions. Ivan went home in despair, his eyes brimming with tears. But when he had told his daughter what had happened, she calmly said:

"Tomorrow, go and catch a hare and a partridge. Both must be alive! You'll have the foal and the hundred silver ducats! Leave it to me!" Ivan did as his daughter said. He had no idea what the two creatures were for, but he trusted in his daughter's wisdom.

On the day of the audience with the Emperor, the palace was thronged with bystanders, waiting for Ivan and his small daughter to arrive. At last, the little girl appeared, draped in a fishing net, riding the hare and holding the partridge in her hand. She was neither naked nor dressed, on foot or on horseback. Scowling, the Emperor told her:

"I said neither bearing gifts nor empty-handed!" At these words, the little girl held out the partridge. The Emperor stretched out his hand to

grasp it, but the bird fluttered into the air. The third condition had been fulfilled. In spite of himself, the Emperor could not help admiring the little girl who had so cleverly passed such a test, and in a gentler voice, he said:

"Is your father terribly poor, and does he desperately need the foal?"

"Oh, yes!" replied the little girl. "We live on the hares he catches in the rivers and the fish he picks from the trees!"

"Aha!" cried the Emperor triumphantly. "So you're not as clever as you seem to be! Whoever heard of hares in the river and fish in the trees!" To which the little girl swiftly replied:

"And whoever heard of a stallion having a foal?" At that, both Emperor and Court burst into peals of laughter. Ivan was immediately given his hundred silver ducats and the foal, and the Emperor proclaimed:

"Only in *my* kingdom could such a wise little girl be born!"

45

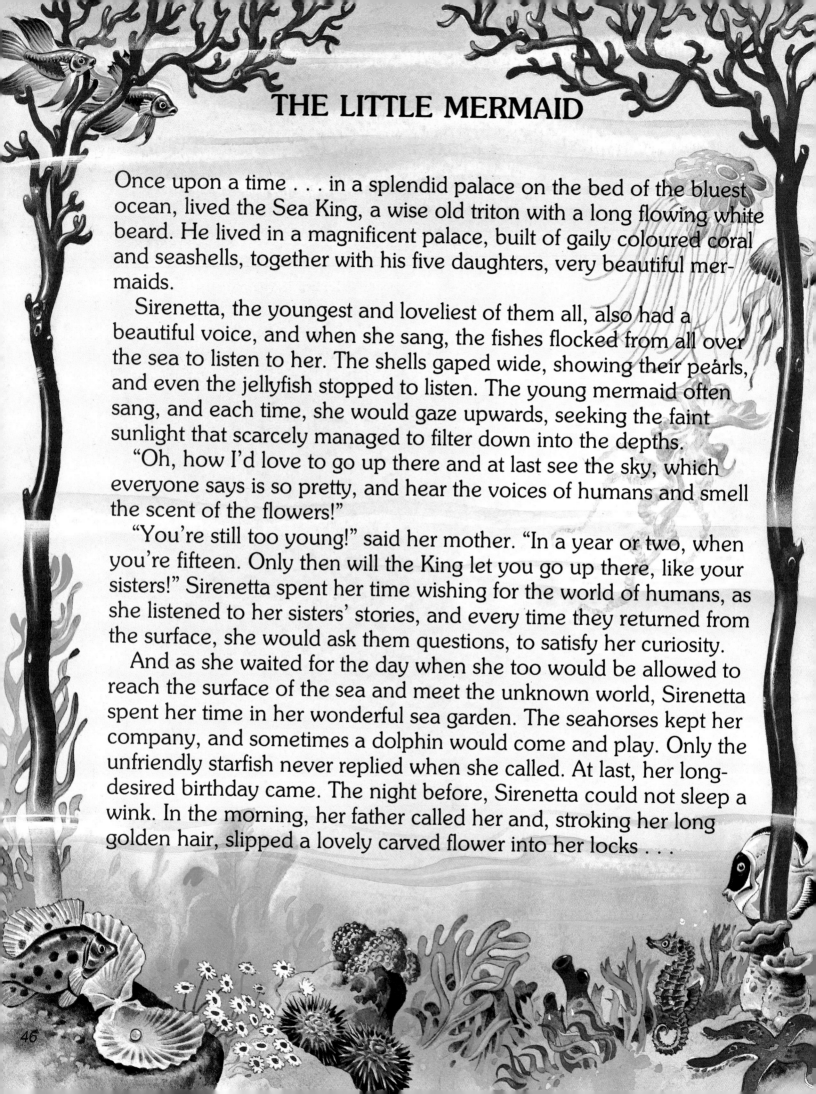

THE LITTLE MERMAID

Once upon a time . . . in a splendid palace on the bed of the bluest ocean, lived the Sea King, a wise old triton with a long flowing white beard. He lived in a magnificent palace, built of gaily coloured coral and seashells, together with his five daughters, very beautiful mermaids.

Sirenetta, the youngest and loveliest of them all, also had a beautiful voice, and when she sang, the fishes flocked from all over the sea to listen to her. The shells gaped wide, showing their pearls, and even the jellyfish stopped to listen. The young mermaid often sang, and each time, she would gaze upwards, seeking the faint sunlight that scarcely managed to filter down into the depths.

"Oh, how I'd love to go up there and at last see the sky, which everyone says is so pretty, and hear the voices of humans and smell the scent of the flowers!"

"You're still too young!" said her mother. "In a year or two, when you're fifteen. Only then will the King let you go up there, like your sisters!" Sirenetta spent her time wishing for the world of humans, as she listened to her sisters' stories, and every time they returned from the surface, she would ask them questions, to satisfy her curiosity.

And as she waited for the day when she too would be allowed to reach the surface of the sea and meet the unknown world, Sirenetta spent her time in her wonderful sea garden. The seahorses kept her company, and sometimes a dolphin would come and play. Only the unfriendly starfish never replied when she called. At last, her long-desired birthday came. The night before, Sirenetta could not sleep a wink. In the morning, her father called her and, stroking her long golden hair, slipped a lovely carved flower into her locks . . .

"There! Now you can go to the surface. You'll breathe air and see the sky. But remember! It's not our world! We can only watch it and admire! We're children of the sea and have no soul, as men do. Be careful and keep away from them; they can only bring bad luck!" In a second, Sirenetta had kissed her father and was darting smoothly towards the surface of the sea. She swam so fast with flicks of her slender tail, that even the fish could not keep up with her.

Suddenly she popped out of the water. How wonderful! For the first time, she saw the great blue sky, in which as dusk began to fall, the first stars were peeping out and twinkling. The sun, already over the horizon, trailed a golden reflection that gently faded on the heaving waves. High overhead, a flock of gulls spotted the little mermaid and greeted her arrival with shrieks of pleasure.

"It's so lovely!" she exclaimed happily. But another nice surprise was in store for her: a ship was slowly sailing towards the rock on which Sirenetta was sitting. The sailors dropped anchor and the ship swayed gently in the calm sea. Sirenetta watched the men go about their work aboard, lighting the lanterns for the night. She could clearly hear their voices.

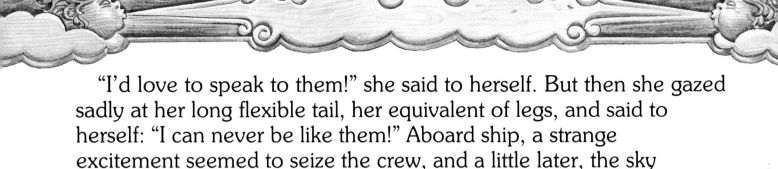

"I'd love to speak to them!" she said to herself. But then she gazed sadly at her long flexible tail, her equivalent of legs, and said to herself: "I can never be like them!" Aboard ship, a strange excitement seemed to seize the crew, and a little later, the sky became a spray of many coloured lights and the crackle of fireworks filled the sky.

"Long live the captain! Hurray for his 20th birthday. Hurray! Hurray . . . many happy returns!" Astonished at all this, the little mermaid caught sight of the young man in whose honour the display was being held. Tall and dignified, he was smiling happily, and Sirenetta could not take her eyes from him. She followed his every movement, fascinated by all that was happening. The party went on, but the sea grew more agitated. Sirenetta anxiously realised that the men were now in danger: an icy wind was sweeping the waves, the ink black sky was torn by flashes of lightning, then a terrible storm broke suddenly over the helpless ship. In vain Sirenetta screamed: "Look out! Beware of the sea . . ." But the howling wind carried her words away, and the rising waves swept over the ship. Amidst the sailors' shouts, masts and sails toppled onto the deck, and with a sinister splintering sound, the ship sank.

By the light of one of the lamps, Sirenetta had seen the young captain fall into the water, and she swam to his rescue. But she could not find him in the high waves and, tired out, was about to give up, when suddenly there he was on the crest of a nearby wave. In an instant, he was swept straight into the mermaid's arms.

The young man was unconscious and the mermaid held his head above water in the stormy sea, in an effort to save his life. She clung to him for hours trying to fight the tiredness that was overtaking her.

Then, as suddenly as it had sprung up, the storm died away. In a grey dawn over a still angry sea, Sirenetta realised thankfully that land lay ahead. Aided by the motion of the waves, she pushed the captain's body onto the shore, beyond the water's edge. Unable herself to walk, the mermaid sat wringing her hands, her tail lapped by the rippling water, trying to warm the young captain with her own body. Then the sound of approaching voices startled Sirenetta and she slipped back into deeper water.

"Come quickly! Quickly!" came a woman's voice in alarm. "There's a man here! Look, I think he's unconscious!" The captain was now in good hands.

"Let's take him up to the castle!"

"No, no! Better get help . . ." And the first thing the young man saw when he opened his eyes again was the beautiful face of the youngest of a group of three ladies.

"Thank you! Thank you . . . for saving my life . . ." he murmured to the lovely unknown lady.

From the sea, Sirenetta watched the man she had snatched from the waves turn towards the castle, without knowing that a mermaid had saved his life. Slowly swimming out to sea, Sirenetta felt that there on the beach she had left behind something she could never bring herself to forget. How wonderful those tremendous hours in the storm had been, as she had battled with the elements. And as she swam down towards her father's palace, her sisters came to meet her, anxious to know what had kept her so long on the surface. Sirenetta started to tell her story, but suddenly a lump came to her throat and, bursting into tears, she fled to her room. She stayed there for days, refusing to see anyone or to touch food. She knew that her love for the young captain was without hope, for she was a mermaid and could never marry a human. Only the Witch of the Deeps could help her. But what price would she have to pay? Sirenetta decided to ask the Witch.

". . . so you want to get rid of your fishy tail, do you? I expect you'd like to have a pair of woman's legs, isn't that so?" said the nasty Witch scornfully, from her cave guarded by a giant squid.

"Be warned!" she went on. "You will suffer horribly, as though a sword were cutting you apart. And every time you place your feet on the earth, you will feel dreadful pain!"

"It doesn't matter!" whispered Sirenetta, with tears in her eyes. "As long as I can go back to him!"

"And that's not all!" exclaimed the Witch. "In exchange for my spell, you must give me your lovely voice. You'll never be able to utter a word again! And don't forget! If the man you love marries someone else, you will not be able to turn into a mermaid again. You will just dissolve in water like the foam on the wave!"

"All right!" said Sirenetta, eagerly taking the little jar holding the magic potion. The Witch had told Sirenetta that the young captain was actually a prince, and the mermaid left the water at a spot not far from the castle. She pulled herself onto the beach, then drank the magic potion. An agonising pain made her faint, and when she came to her senses, she could mistily see the face she loved, smiling down at her.

The witch's magic had worked the spell, for the prince had felt a strange desire to go down to the beach, just as Sirenetta was arriving. There he had stumbled on her, and recalling how he too had once been washed up on the shore, gently laid his cloak over the still body, cast up by the waves.

"Don't be frightened!" he said quickly. "You're quite safe! Where have you come from?" But Sirenetta was now dumb and could not reply, so the young man softly stroked her wet cheek.

"I'll take you to the castle and look after you," he said. In the days that followed, the

mermaid started a new life. She wore splendid dresses and often went out on horseback with the prince. One evening, she was invited to a great ball at Court. However, as the Witch had foretold, every movement and each step she took was torture. Sirenetta bravely put up with her suffering, glad to be allowed to stay near her beloved prince. And though she could not speak to him, he was fond of her and showered kindness on her, to her great joy. However, the young man's heart really belonged to the unknown lady he had seen as he lay on the shore, though he had never met her since, for she had returned at once to her own land.

Even when he was in the company of Sirenetta, fond of her as he was, the unknown lady was always in his thoughts. And the little mermaid, guessing instinctively that she was not his true love, suffered even more.

She often crept out of the castle at night, to weep by the seashore. Once she thought she could spy her sisters rise from the water and wave at her, but this made her feel sadder than ever.

Fate, however, had another surprise in store. From the Castle ramparts one day, a huge ship was sighted sailing into the harbour. Together with Sirenetta, the prince went down to meet it. And who stepped from the vessel, but the unknown lady who had been for so long in the prince's heart. When he saw her, he rushed to greet her. Sirenetta felt herself turn to stone and a painful feeling pierced her heart: she was about to lose the prince for ever. The unknown lady too had never forgotten the young man she had found on the beach, and soon after, he asked her to marry him. Since she too was in love, she happily said "yes".

A few days after the wedding, the happy couple were invited to go for a voyage on the huge ship, which was still in the harbour. Sirenetta too went on board, and the ship set sail. Night fell, and sick at heart over the loss of the prince, Sirenetta went on deck. She remembered the Witch's prophecy, and was now ready to give up her life and dissolve in the sea. Suddenly she heard a cry from the water and dimly saw her sisters in the darkness.

". . . Sirenetta! Sirenetta! It's us . . . your sisters! We've heard all about what happened! Look! Do you see this knife? It's magic! The Witch gave it to us in exchange for our hair. Take it! Kill the prince before dawn, and you will become a mermaid again and forget all your troubles!"

As though in a trance, Sirenetta clasped the knife and entered the cabin where the prince and his bride lay asleep. But as she gazed at the young man's sleeping face, she simply blew him a furtive kiss, before running back on deck. When dawn broke, she threw the knife into the sea. Then she shot a parting glance at the world she was leaving behind, and dived into the waves, ready to turn into the foam of the sea from whence she had come, and vanish.

As the sun rose over the horizon, it cast a long golden ray of light across the sea, and in the chilly water, Sirenetta turned towards it for the last time. Suddenly, as though by magic, a mysterious force drew her out of the water, and she felt herself lifted high into the sky. The clouds were tinged with pink, the sea rippled in the early morning breeze, and the little mermaid heard a whisper through the tinkling of bells: "Sirenetta, Sirenetta! Come with us . . ."

"Who are you?" asked the mermaid, surprised to find she had recovered the use of her voice. "Where am I?"

"You're with us in the sky. We're the fairies of the air! We have no soul as men do, but our task is to help them. We take amongst us only those who have shown kindness to men!"

Greatly touched, Sirenetta looked down over the sea towards the prince's ship, and felt tears spring to her eyes. The fairies of the air whispered to her: "Look! The earth flowers are waiting for our tears to turn into the morning dew! Come along with us . . ."